Other Oxford Books
by Val Biro

Hungarian Folk-tales
The Magic Doctor
Jack and the Robbers
(*text by Jill Bennett*)
The Hobyahs
The Pied Piper of Hamelin
The Donkey that Sneezed
The Odd-Job Man and the Thousand-mile Boots
(*text by Jean Kenward*)
Jack and the Beanstalk
The Three Little Pigs
What's Up the Coconut Tree?
(*text by A. H. Benjamin*)
The Three Billy-Goats Gruff
The Show-Off Mouse
(*text by A. H. Benjamin*)
Lazy Jack
Hansel and Gretel
Goldilocks and the Three Bears

To Katie,
my Little Red Riding Hood,
with love

OXFORD
UNIVERSITY PRESS
Great Clarendon Street, Oxford OX2 6DP
Oxford University Press is a department of the University of Oxford.
It furthers the University's objective of excellence in research, scholarship,
and education by publishing worldwide in
Oxford New York
Athens Auckland Bangkok Bogotá Buenos Aires Calcutta
Cape Town Chennai Dar es Salaam Delhi Florence Hong Kong Istanbul
Karachi Kuala Lumpur Madrid Melbourne Mexico City Mumbai
Nairobi Paris São Paulo Singapore Taipei Tokyo Toronto Warsaw
with associated companies in Berlin Ibadan

First published 2000

British Library Cataloguing in Publication Data available
ISBN 0-19-272392-8
Printed in Hong Kong

Little Red Riding Hood

Retold and illustrated by

Val Biro

OXFORD
UNIVERSITY PRESS

ONCE there was a little girl called Katie.
She lived in a village near the wood, and each time she went out she wore a little red cape with a hood.
It was her favourite and she wore it every day.
So everybody called her Little Red Riding Hood.

One Saturday her mother said,
'Little Red Riding Hood,
Grandma is not very well,
so go and take this letter
to her. There is also a
fruit cake and a bottle of
elderberry wine in this basket.
And be careful as you go through
the wood. Take this stick,
too, just in case.'

So Little Red Riding Hood
took the basket, with the
letter in it, and picked up
the stick. She waved goodbye
to her mother and set off
towards the wood.

Soon she was walking along the woodland path. Sunshine twinkled through the leaves, birds sang, and squirrels played in the branches. Bluebells and primroses bordered the path and everything looked peaceful and bright.

But deep in the dark forest there lived a wolf.
A big and wicked wolf who was always hungry. Today he was hungrier than ever, so when he saw Little Red Riding Hood walking along the path, his eyes flashed.
'Here comes my breakfast!' he muttered, licking his lips.

Little Red Riding Hood knew nothing of this wolf. She walked on, enjoying the sunshine and admiring the flowers.

'I know,' she said, 'I'll pick some for Grandma to cheer her up!'

So she picked some bluebells here and some primroses there, until she had gathered enough flowers for a lovely bunch. Then, with her basket and stick, she continued on her way.

Unfortunately, the letter had dropped out of the basket and it remained lying there, on the path.

But not for long. When the wicked wolf saw it,
he snatched it up and sprang back into the shadows.
There he read the address on the letter:
To Grandma, By-the-Bridge Cottage, Woodside.

'Ah-ha-ha!' cackled the wolf. 'So that's where she's going! I'll get there before her and have two meals for the price of one!'

The hungry wolf ran like the wind right across the forest. He knew a short cut and he got to Grandma's cottage by the bridge in no time at all.

The wolf knocked on the door *toc-toc*.

'Who's there?' asked Grandma.

'Your granddaughter,' replied the wolf in a piping voice. 'And I have brought you a letter and a basket with a bottle of elderberry wine.'

'Come in, my dear,' said Grandma. 'I'm in bed but the door's open.'

The wicked wolf flung it wide open, stormed into the cottage, and . . .

. . . instantly he leapt upon the bed and ate up Grandma in one big mouthful—GULP.

Then he shut the door, put Grandma's nightcap on his head and climbed into bed. He pulled the sheet over his face and settled down to wait for Little Red Riding Hood.

Soon she came and knocked on the door, *toc-toc.*

'Who's there?' asked a gruff voice. It scared Little Red Riding Hood at first, but then she thought that Grandma must have a very sore throat.

So she said, 'It is your granddaughter and I have brought you a basket from Mum and some flowers.'

The wolf softened his voice the best he could and said, 'Come in, my dear. I'm in bed but the door's open.'

So Little Red Riding Hood pushed it open and went in.

The room was dark and all she could see of Grandma was her nightcap among the pillows.

'Come a little closer,' croaked the voice from the bed, 'so that I can see you.'

Little Red Riding Hood opened the curtain to let in more light, and went closer. Grandma didn't *sound* like herself at all, she thought.

Now that it was lighter, she could see that Grandma didn't *look* like herself, either.

'Oh, Grandma, what big ears you have!' she cried.

'All the better to hear you with,' came the reply.

Little Red Riding Hood crept closer still.

'Oh, Grandma, what big eyes you have!'

'All the better to see you with!'

Little Red Riding Hood gripped her stick and took another step.

'Oh, Grandma, what big teeth you have!'

'All the better to EAT you with!' cried the wicked wolf and . . .

. . . he sprang at Little Red Riding Hood with his mouth wide open.

But quick as a flash she jammed the stick between his gaping jaws and propped them firmly apart.

The wolf could not shut his mouth, however hard he tried, so he just sat on the bed, looking foolish. Just then, Little Red Riding Hood heard a muffled cry from the wolf's tummy. It was Grandma! So quickly she called down the wolf's open mouth, 'Grandma, you can come out now!'

Out came Grandma safe
and sound, though a bit dazed.
When she saw the wolf, she grabbed
her broom and cried angrily,
'So there you are! I'll give you
eating people, my lad! Here's
a lesson you won't forget
in a hurry!'

She swung the broom above her head and beat the wicked wolf *biff-baff-biff* so hard that he staggered out of the door in sheer terror and ran back into the wood, howling.

Grandma ran after him, waving her broom, but by then the wolf was far away, howling in the distance.

Just then the gamekeeper came by, riding his bike across the bridge.

'There goes the wolf,' cried Grandma, urgently. 'He nearly ate me! Go on, after him!'

And off rode the gamekeeper in
hot pursuit, cycling furiously.

'Phew!' said Grandma. 'That was a close thing. But I feel a lot better now!' And she took Little Red Riding Hood to the kitchen for a slice of Mum's fruit cake—and a glass of elderberry wine.

And the wicked wolf? Well, the gamekeeper probably caught him. If not, then the wolf must have decided to keep well away from Grandma's *biff-baff-biff* broom and that crafty Little Red Riding Hood.

At any rate, nobody has ever seen him again.